THE GIFT OF YOU

GRAVESIDE READS VOL. 1
ISSUE 5

CHLOE YORK

For those brave enough to put cracks in your porcelain—just don't make it literal.

The Gift of you

CHAPTER 1

Pinpricks of ice pelt my cheeks as I stumble my way to Miriam's massive front door. Gloved fingers brushing the spiky sprigs of a cedar wreath, I take hold of the door knocker, dropping the brass ball with one solid *thunk*, followed by another. My nostrils sting with each inhale, breath pulsing between my lips in wraith-like tendrils.

I release yet another inward prayer that Mother won't awaken and find me gone, that the laudanum I teaspooned into her warm milk will be enough.

Everleigh Manor appears especially alive tonight, all the gas lanterns ablaze. On my way here, I followed that light like a north star through the wildflower field, now a slumbering tangle of frost-tinged grass that made each crunching step from home feel like a delicious, tangible rebellion. But now that I'm actually here—alone —at this hour, on her doorstep, with but a single wall separating us, my courage has fled.

What would Mother say? What would Frederick—

When the door opens, I expect Mrs. Stark, the housekeeper,

with her stony stare, but instead it's Miriam flooding the brick stoop in amber warmth.

"Cecile! You came!" she exclaims, grasping my arm and tugging me into the marble-floored foyer before I can alter my mind with more unwanted hypotheticals.

The delicate aroma of cinnamon and butter coax saliva across my tongue. I brush snow from my boots before removing my coat and gloves and hanging them on a mahogany coat rack. Through winter-stung eyes, I study Miriam. Her gown is a creamy white embroidered with lace in the same icy blue shade as her eyes. And draped around her swan-like neck are the pearls I had my scullery maid deliver to her this afternoon.

"If I hadn't, you would have dragged me here yourself," I say, still catching my breath from the walk and how beautiful Miri looks in those pearls, just as I knew she would the moment I saw them in the shop window during one of my rare unchaperoned strolls with Frederick.

They will be the perfect present for Mother, I lied, uncertain why I felt the need to.

"You're lucky I didn't," she teases, touching the necklace. Her eyes flash to mine. "Shame on you for not giving them to me yourself."

I blush, finding sudden fascination with the banister beyond her shoulder. Anywhere I can avoid looking directly into that perfect face and that crystalline gaze. Like the harshest winter sunlight that at one instant turns from welcome warmth to searing blindness. That's what Miri reminds me of at this moment. Alone together for the first time in...

How long has it been?

"I have been busy," I try.

A tense beat.

"With Frederick?" she asks, voice tight.

"Yes," I say, casting my gaze to the floor. "He called on me again this morning. I could not refuse."

I wait for her to say more, but just as quickly, she brightens, taking my hand and pulling me toward the grand dining room.

Since her parents took ill and passed away last year, this house and everything in it belongs to her, a team of clerks managing her small fortune while she is free to pursue her watercolor painting and impressive doll collection. Despite the loss she suffered, I cannot help but envy her life. When Mother dies, the entirety of our family fortune will go to my younger brother. Marrying Frederick Grayson is the only way I'll have even a portion of what Miriam Everleigh has.

A luscious spread is laid on the table before us. Not like it was in the old days when her parents were still alive. Miriam's tastes are fine, yet subdued. Less extravagant than theirs was. But here Miri's topped the table with pastries, dried fruits, even a crystal decanter of rich dark wine that flares like a many-faceted ruby in the candlelight.

Two decadent place settings are situated directly across from each other.

Close. Intimate.

I take the farthest chair and strain my ears for any telltale footsteps in the upper floors or a clatter of dishes from the kitchen, but the house is silent save for Miriam's rapid breathing.

"Are we—?" I begin, spreading the embroidered linen napkin across my lap. "Where are the staff this evening?"

"I sent them home," Miriam says with a sly grin as she plucks a shriveled purple fig and raises it to her full lips.

I blink.

"But doesn't Mrs. Stark have a room upstairs?"

Miriam lifts one shoulder, the lace at her neckline shifting fetchingly down with the motion. I scan her exposed clavicle, the swell of her curves beneath her cream-colored gown before catching myself. The cinnamon pastry is tasteless glue between my teeth while I work to evade studying her too closely.

"I no longer keep live-in servants," says Miri, plucking the lid off the decanter and splashing blood-red liquid first into my glass, then hers. The tendons in her graceful neck flutter as she drinks. "And as for Mrs. Stark, well." Another sip. "You know we never did see eye to eye. I let her go months ago."

She frowns, the meaning behind the expression all too obvious. That during my courtship with Frederick, I have lost touch with my best friend. So much so that I have overlooked such a significant occurrence as old Mrs. Stark's dismissal. But any guilt I feel is overshadowed by this fresh, dangerous knowledge—that Miri and I are, for the first time, entirely and utterly alone.

"I did not know," I say at last, my voice small, abashed. I down my wine in three considerate pulls. The drink's swift burn hums through my head and deepens the heat in my cheeks. "Is it wicked to admit I never cared for her? Ever since we were girls."

Miriam titters behind her hand.

"She was a deplorable old bitch."

The boldness of her language widens my eyes for a beat before an easy laugh replaces it. It has always felt like this with Miriam Everleigh. Equal parts affronted and fascinated by her crass fearlessness. The desire to *be* her. To leech even a fraction of that boldness and weaponize it against Mother's cruel tongue and—

Stop. No more sinful thoughts. Mother is ill. She deserves my respect, my obedience. I should consider myself fortunate I have a parent who still lives, especially after Miriam lost both of hers.

"Have you eaten enough, my lovely?" she asks.

"Yes," I lie. "Thank you, Miri."

"Then come," Miriam says, dabbing her napkin to the edges of her shapely mouth. She rises demurely, an elegant dance to her commonplace movements that offsets the vulgarity inside. "I have a surprise for you."

CHAPTER 2

Miriam is incandescent even among the scant gaslit sconces dotting the long hallway. I try unsuccessfully to match her assured swaying walk as she leads me toward the parlor.

The snug, red-wallpapered, lavish sitting room, is now brimming with Christmas finery. So many afternoons in our youth we spent cross-legged on that plush window seat with our embroidery and books. All the lazy evenings we sipped tea and divulged unspeakable wishes to one another. That we could attend university like my brother, Theodore. That we could travel independently without fear of harassment.

But there is one secret, all-consuming desire I will never divulge to Miriam Everleigh. Especially not to Miriam Everleigh.

"Sit," she says, gesturing to the loveseat beside the Christmas tree.

Lost in my head, I absently note the roaring fire Miri lays another log on top of before prodding the stack with a poker. The wind roars outside, the blizzard picking up. I won't allow myself to think about how difficult the storm will be to traverse when it is time to return home.

I obey her command and sit, watching her leave the fireplace to stoop beneath the tree and retrieve a package topped with a silken black bow. I slow my breathing to steady the swift wingbeats fluttering in my chest. The sharp aroma of pine and smoke tingles in my nostrils, a welcome distraction from her nearness. She stops in front of me with a playful bounce of her heels and presents the gift with an eager grin.

"What is it?" I ask, taking the box. It is long and narrow and brings to mind the twin coffins they placed Miri's mother and father in before they were interred. The blank stare of her once fiery gaze obscured by a mourning veil at the well-attended funeral. A shadow of herself as I took her hand and felt her firm grip overtake mine. Even at her worst moment, that same strength she always had... I loved her all the more for it.

When she sinks beside me on the sofa, electrifyingly close, my skin tingles with her proximity and it takes all I have in me not to shift away as our arms brush. The artfully wrapped package is heavy atop my thighs. I focus on its weight instead of her touch.

"Open it."

With an anticipatory shiver, I slide off the bow and unfurl the paper with all the care and respect its fine wrapping demands. I've no doubt Miri wrapped it herself. Measured the damask patterned paper, sliced it with silver shears, folded the edges clean with her long, elegant fingers.

With an impatient huff, she reaches across me to yank open the paper. Two jagged sides split violently apart, the resulting *riiiip* coaxing a sharp breath through my teeth.

"But you worked so hard on this," I protest.

"The presentation is not the precious part," she grins, easing back. "Now hurry. I want you to see what's inside."

Returning her smile, I oblige her.

She never stops watching me. Not when I run my questing

palms across the lacquered box's carved lid. Not when I take hold of its sides and raise its hinged lid.

I loose an exhale that rattles my ribcage, giddily anticipating what might be inside. A new book? A china vase for collecting wildflowers when spring comes?

What I find instead drags a low hum from my stomach.

It is a doll, crafted in my exact likeness.

The doll with my face peers from its wrapping-paper womb, all gilded curls and huge brown eyes. Entranced, I lift it from the box, stroking my thumb along its cool, glassy cheek.

"She's you," Miriam says, brushing aside a strand of hair caught in my lashes. The tender contact threatens to overtake me like the dense ivy still clinging to the walls of Everleigh Manor.

"I can see that," I tell her, voice low as I settle deeper into the sofa, training my focus only on the doll and not Miri's face mere inches from mine.

The doll's nose is pert with a slight upturn at the tip. Its lips are full and pink. There are freckles, beige pinpricks that appear to have been dabbed on with a single hair in place of a paint brush. It isn't only that the doll has my hair and eye color. It has been molded and shaped as my precise small-scale likeness, down to the little mole high upon its left cheekbone.

Miriam's smile has a glint of familiar mischief in it. It's the smile she favored me with the day we met, in the springtime of my eleventh year. I'd resolved to run away from home, become a fae creature of the wilds, free from Mother's biting insults and impossible expectations. With nothing but a stolen wedge of soft white cheese and a stale dinner roll tucked in a kerchief, I set out first thing in the morning, drawn inexorably to the ocean of flowers flanking the forest.

Pink astor, blazing star, butterfly weed. All were known to me from books, my only companions. And in that field, twirling and singing without abandon among the circling bees and dandelion fluff, was a girl. She had a crown of daisies woven into her unbound black hair, the hem of her dress coated in clinging seedlings. And when her eyes found mine, I knew I was exactly where I belonged.

A sanctuary and a certain kind of Hell.

For the wild stirrings Miriam Everleigh elicited in my belly from the moment she took my hand in that field of flowers and dragged me along to our adulthoods. For how in moments like this, enveloped by her earthy scent, tracking the rise and fall of her breathing near enough to match it, I long for something I'm too afraid to name.

"It's not just any doll, my lovely," she continues, resting her hand atop mine atop the doll's lap. My chest hitches as her touch remains, my ribs straining above a dull thrum. That want, that *ache.* "It is *you.*"

As I lift a questioning brow at her, the doll's face flashes in my periphery, the painted slashes of its eyebrows drawing together. There and gone in an instant, leaving nothing amiss on its static features when I regard it full on.

"Are we not too old for playthings?" I ask with a dry swallow, sliding my hand from hers. I busy myself with straightening the sleeves on the doll's red dress.

Miriam smiles impishly. Her pearl necklace flashes in the firelight, along with her teeth. Silvery strands of tinsel sway in the pungent evergreen among its array of hanging ornaments and baubles.

Every Christmas needs presents, she explained over tea last year while sour-faced Mrs. Stark hovered in the corner dusting the same bookshelf for over an hour. *And every present needs a tree to go under.*

Christmases in Everleigh Manor were once grand affairs. String quartets, silk gowns and satin ribbons, endless puddings and sweets, an enormous turkey browned and crisp on a banquet table overflowing with garlands of pine and imported citrus fruits. Miri and I lingered in the upstairs nursery with the other children, sneaking apple tarts with buttery crusts that melted on our tongues like the richest unspoken secrets.

This is to be our last Christmas together before I marry Frederick and begin my new life at his townhouse in the city. My stomach twists at the unwelcome thought. By next year, nights like this will be a distant memory.

But tonight, in Miriam's lavish candle-lit sitting room, the dark windows ensconced with powdery snowfall, we were the only two creatures in existence before the doll joined us. This miniaturized twin of me. This gift of me.

"It is no toy, Cecile," Miriam smirks. "And I doubt dolls have ever amused you. I know you much better than that, my lovely."

Outside, the wind howls, the blizzard intensifying. I turn the doll this way and that, a tingle edging along my skin where Miriam's gaze strikes it. She's right, of course. I never played with dolls as a child. I preferred the magic of my own imagination or the company of a fairy story. Miriam, on the other hand, loved dolls. Collected them from the finest toymakers. Fashioned her own out of twigs and scraps of old dresses. Brushed their hair. Polished their tiny shoes. Whispered over them. Poppets, she called them. Her silent friends.

This doll is as fitting a gift from her as any as my own childhood comes to its end. Next Christmas, I will be a wife. There will be no more clover crowns, no more fairy tales, no more Everleigh Manor.

No more Miriam.

"Enlighten me then," I say with a forced smile as my throat fills with cotton. Another flicker of movement on the doll's lips, there and gone. The lantern light catches across its shiny ceramic face. My face. "If not just a toy, then what?"

"Haven't you been listening?" she teases. "It is *you*."

I chuckle, tamping the urge to shift nearer to her on the tufted cushion.

"Miri, please. No riddles. It is late and I must be getting back. The storm…"

Miriam leans in, a spill of black hair loosening from its pins.

She smells of pine and citrus, potent and sweet. She takes the doll. Whispers across its golden curls. As she does, a warm breeze caresses my cheek—a draft from the fireplace perhaps.

She adopts a strange look then. Wolfish. Provocative. The skin pinches between her brows, her jawline rigid, her pale eyes hardening to ice. I blink, a surge of unease carving through my want, but something else, too.

Exhilaration.

Excitement.

Miri could be a goddess of war. An eldritch fairy queen.

"Back to what?" she challenges, her words as cutting as her bared slash of a smile. "That monstrous woman who calls herself a mother? That complete bore of a fiancé? To a future you don't even want?"

My spine straightens, nostrils flaring open, my heart a wounded bird fluttering behind my ribs. My enchantment ebbs, replaced by confused hurt.

"What are you saying?"

"I speak the truth, Cecile," Miriam says, softening. "Now be still for me."

"Miri, what—"

She presses her lips against the doll's forehead, tender and deliberate, her eyes trained on mine. I gasp, touching my own forehead, where an invisible pressure tingles on my skin.

A trick. Suggestive thinking. It must be.

"We both know that place is not your home," she continues, eyes glinting. "You belong here, Cecile. With me."

When Miriam kisses the doll's tiny parted lips, I feel it, too. There and gone. A teasing contact, whisper light.

"Miri..." I breathe, eyes wide. My lungs strain against my corset, unable to draw in enough air. "What is happening?"

"Happy Christmas, my lovely," she says, her mischievous facade receding at last. Trapping her bottom lip beneath her teeth, she lifts the doll's skirts. Brushes her finger along its polished white leg.

I shiver at the contact across my own calf.

"How?" I pant. "Miri—"

She shushes me, gathering the doll's dress about its stuffed fabric waist. When she presses into the smooth, formless place between the doll's legs, I cry out, back arching against the embroidered loveseat. She rubs in a tight semicircle, her predatory smile returning.

This is witchcraft. This is evil. This is...

Perfection.

CHAPTER 3

Through the hazy cloud of my horrified astonishment, Miriam's scent chokes me, and God help me, I want it to. I want all of her. Her flesh on my flesh. Her touch on me. Not that accursed doll, but *me* and—

No. For the sake of us both, I must be stronger than this.

You're so good, Ceci, Miriam used to tell me. *My unfailing moral compass.*

Swallowing my pleasurable moans, I squeeze my legs shut, fighting against the sensation, against *her,* but she's relentless. I must remember who I am, that it is not too late, that I can still save us both.

"Stop," I choke, wringing my fingers through my skirts, a hot flush gathering in my chest and flooding into my face. "Miri, please. Stop this."

You spend a lot of time with that woman.

Frederick. Arm in arm as he guided me down cobblestone streets with Anna the scullery maid trailing close behind.

Do you not find it odd that she chooses to live alone? he

continued after noting my anxious silence. *She is a pretty thing and exceedingly wealthy. She must have her pick of suitors.*

Miriam is...selective, I said at last, followed by a tactful, *She will find the right man someday, just as I have.*

The lie—both of them—tasted like salt between my teeth. Yet still I reveled in the safety of Frederick's grasp tightening about my shoulders, my fortune and comfort secured.

"Cecile," Miriam whispers over the doll, never once easing up on her touches. "My Cecile."

Unseemly, that girl. Mother, stifling a wet cough, handkerchief pressed to her lips. *Why her parents never managed to tame her, I will never know. Running that fine household any way she pleases, not even trying to secure a husband. It's obscene.*

I looked up from my horticulture book to find Mother's wilting gaze upon me, as if I were a common garden slug on her prized roses.

I thank the good Lord every day that girl didn't ruin your prospects. I don't care how much money she has. She is an uncouth trollop who broke her poor parents' hearts. Another crackling, wet cough. *No doubt they're turning over in their graves to see her now.*

While wild and wretched anger seared through me, I only managed a curt nod of agreement before returning to my reading.

"I have wanted this for so long," Miriam breathes, climbing over my helpless form.

"N—no," I stammer, dragging myself upright.

Heart thundering, fighting against my combined ecstasy and shame, I snatch the doll from her and clutch it securely to my chest. I shuffle away like a caged animal until my back strikes the sofa's armrest.

"What do you think you're doing?" I snap through labored breaths.

"It's not a sin if I don't touch you," she says, her smile unfaltering.

I squeeze the doll harder, stroking its hair in an attempt to ground myself. I don't register my own touches as I did Miriam's. My dearest friend's violating—yet so intoxicating—touches. Shadows lengthen over us as the blizzard rages outside. In the guttering firelight, she is beautiful in the way that all frightening things are. Angular. Sharp. Forbidden.

"Have you ever been touched that way before, my lovely?" she continues, edging closer until her face hovers over mine. "Has Frederick even kissed you?"

My blush deepens. It doesn't matter what I think of Frederick now. One day, he and I will come to love each other in the way that Miriam and I cannot because she is a woman and I am a woman and if Mother ever found out about tonight or God forbid, Frederick—

"I'm going now," I manage, cradling the doll as if it's my very soul. "Please, Miri. I will forget this night and I beg you to do the same." With shaking hands, I shove the doll at her, rebuking her gift. "Whatever trick this is, whatever conjurer's charm you've employed, remove it. Take this horrid thing back. I..." A sting behind my eyes, a knot trapped in my throat. "I do not desire you."

She blinks those pale eyes at the doll in her hands. Her shoulders hitch as she hefts a sigh. The blizzard picks up in intensity, howling winds rattling the windows in their panes. The Christmas tree rustles. At our feet, the cavernous innards of the package the doll arrived in are an open mouth framed by jagged paper teeth.

"You may lie to yourself," Miriam says at last, "but you cannot lie to me."

When she tosses the doll on the cushion behind her, my own body registers the contact as a breathtaking jolt across my back. Miriam clasps my hands in hers, vulnerable in a way I've never seen her before. Her grip is strong, grinding my knuckles together. The pearls I gifted her clack against her breastbone as her desperate eyes latch onto mine.

"Let me free you, Cecile. Take care of you as when we were children. He cannot make you happy like I will. Frederick is just another cage. Another jailer, just like your mother. Like my parents were." Her grip tightens. "But I freed myself from them and I can do the same for you. You have only but to ask."

Trembling, I tear loose from Miriam and stand, heeled boots sinking in the floral rug. She rises with me, that wildness I always admired visible in every facet of her diamond eyes and angular cheekbones. She is a sorceress, an agent of the devil on this most holy night and she would drag me with her into his clutches. I never knew this woman at all.

"No, Miri," I plead, twisting toward the grand foyer. "I'm leaving now. When you've come to your senses, you'll—"

I cry out when she yanks me by my wrist and tosses me to the loveseat. The doll bounces in my wake just before she takes it into her arms like an errant child. Miriam's chest rises and falls, twin rivers carving down each rosy cheek.

"Admit it," she says, her voice hushed, inflectionless. Without preamble, she winds her fingers into the doll's golden curls and rips several strands loose.

I cry out, my scalp aflame. Wisps of golden thread flutter past my eyes. My own hair, torn from the root.

CHAPTER 4

My eyes burn with unshed tears, a scream caught in my chest.

"Admit that you love me," Miriam presses, digging her nails into the doll's soft belly. I groan at the sensation of dull blades jabbing my skin, bruising and punishing.

"Miriam," I cry, doubled over, hugging myself. "Don't—"

"Stop denying us!" Miriam shrieks, her composure dropping like a heavy curtain at the last opera we attended and silently snickered the entire way through even as Mother glared at us.

This is not that woman.

This is not my Miri.

Shuddering, chest hitching, I lean forward and tear the doll away from her. I dart toward the foyer with it, storm be damned. I need to leave this place, put as much distance between myself and her crazed obsession as I can before—

With a low snarl, she cuts me off, placing her small yet powerful body in front of the door.

"Move," I say, ashamed of how wavery the command comes out.

"Only if you give me the doll," she counters.

I freed myself from them and I can do the same for you.

The suddenness of Lord and Lady Everleigh's illness. How it took them both in a matter of days. How frightened I was for Miriam's health and that of her staff after their untimely passing. Yet by some miracle, the sickness failed to touch anyone else in her household.

"Did you kill them?" I can't help but ask. Because I need to despise her now. If I have any hope of fleeing her, I must forget the girl I thought I knew, the girl I—

"I did not," Miriam replies, both hands raised as if I am a wounded creature she is trying not to spook into running.

"Then what did you mean before? How did you free yourself from them?"

"There will be time enough to explain," she says, whatever collectedness she might have had giving way to an urgent malice. "Let's return to the sitting room, yes? Let's talk. Give me a chance to fix this. That's all I ask."

"Just let me go," I beg with a tentative forward step. "And I promise, because we are—*were* friends, I will grant you the courtesy of never speaking of this night to anyone. But if you so much as touch me again, I'll—"

"Think, Cecile," she says. "You can't go out there. Not in this storm. Now come. Give me the doll and—"

Without thinking, I twist toward the stairwell. If memory serves, the upstairs bedrooms are equipped with thumb-turn locks. If I can barricade myself in one of them, I can wait out the storm or for Miriam to return to her senses, whichever comes first.

I will not fight her. Even after all this, the thought of harming her is more than I can bear. So while every instinct wants to drive me outside and take my chances in the merciless snow, my crazed desperation makes the decision for me. My scalp throbs where Miriam ripped out my hair without touching me, the pain somehow second to the ghost of her fingers between my thighs as I rush up the grand staircase.

"Cecile!" Miriam cries over the pounding of our feet. "Stop!"

The doll's tangled hair tickles the hollow place between my throat and chin as she bounces in my arms. I don't dare sneak a glance to see how close Miriam might be. I brace for fingers to clasp my shoulder or wind about my ankle to drag me down with her, but there's not so much as a whisper of sensation as I crest the top step and observe the wall of doors waiting to harbor myself and my porcelain doppelgänger.

"Cecile!" Miriam roars at my back.

Tag, you're it!

A flash of vibrant memory. Miriam and I as children chasing one another up and down these very halls to the chagrin of the maids and of course, Mrs. Stark, who was convinced we would damage the fine vases and mahogany tables and expensive portraits lining the walls. My steadfast desire to be the good, proper girl Mother trained me to be would always cause my pace to slow, whereas Miriam had no such fears. As a result, she always, *always* caught me.

I can feel her overeager shove on my spine even now.

You're it, Ceci! Now you have to tag me back.

Stifling a sob, I hurl myself through the first open doorway I come to and slam it closed just as Miriam's harried form materializes in front of it. With impressive speed, I take hold of the latch and twist it to the locked position just before Miriam slams her entire weight into the heavy wooden door.

It reverberates in its frame with a sharp thud that forces me back, clinging to the doll with all that I am. Absently, I rub the sore spot on my head where Miriam plucked out our hair and straighten the dress she raised to expose her and—

It is you, Miri said.

The doorknob shifts back and forth, back and forth with intermittent thwacks upon the door itself.

"Cecile, please," Miriam tries. Even muffled, the anguish in her words drags a whimper from my own lips. "Please come out of there. I promise I won't hurt you."

"You already hurt me," I cry.

"Please," she presses. "I'm sorry. I—I don't know what came over me."

Clenching my eyes shut, I tune out her words and retreat deeper into the bedroom. *Her* bedroom, I realize. The immense canopy bed, the row of windows displaying a rising mound of snow on the sills, and the surest sign of all: the *dolls*.

They occupy the entire far wall. Shelves upon shelves of them in all shapes and sizes. Some would fit into the palm of my hand while others are as tall as I and in all manner of dress and style. Fine gowns and jewels in miniature. Patchwork rags and burlap. Stitched and sculpted. Twigs and clay. Some without faces, others with glassy-eyed stares that try their hardest to be alive, to *exist*.

"Please unlock the door," Miriam continues, her voice a faraway afterthought with the countless imitations of humanity I have found myself confronted with. They are all that is real to me now, the doll Miriam gifted me the only solidity I have to cling to.

CHAPTER 5

The new stillness in the air has a ringing to it. I am barely aware that I've not heard a peep from Miriam since her last plea. Has she given up? Slumped against the door to wait me out? Where is she?

The noise is faint at first. A close-mouthed grunt. Testing, searching. I hardly heard it over the insistent howling blizzard. The doll and I seek the shadowed planes of Miriam's bedroom for its source.

I let out a sharp cry when a figure materializes by the doorway, only to follow the scream with a crazed giggle. It is only my reflection in the vanity mirror. My once-smooth tresses are a shock of golden tangles, my cheeks ruddy and wet with fearful tears. I keep one arm clamped over the doll as another sound joins the first.

"*Mmph,*" it says.

My gaze flicks about the room, scanning everything and nothing, feeling increasingly foolish. The wardrobe contains nothing but Miriam's dresses. Their scent caresses me before I get up to slam the doors closed. Like a child seeking monsters, I peer under the bed only to find dead space, as I knew I would. Because I know what's making the sound. I just don't want to accept it.

No, as much as my body and mind refuse to give credence to it, there is but one place from which the sounds can be coming.

The overflowing racks of dolls.

An audience of glass eyes and formless faces suck in a collective breath at my approach. Unthinking, every fiber of me giving way to slow, syrupy dread, I lay my own doll atop the vanity seat before straining my ears for another tell-tale rustle or groan, hoping against all hope that it won't come.

Unfortunately, it does.

A low, piercing wail that turns to many. A hellish chorus of misery. It takes me a moment to realize I've joined them. Hands clasped to the sides of my head to drown them out, I crumble to the carpeted floor with my knees drawn to my heaving chest in a childish repose.

The dolls cry. The dolls feel. The dolls *live*. And it is far more than my sanity can withstand. But I must collect myself now. I have to escape this place, escape Miriam—my Miri—the only person who ever made me feel safe, wanted, *loved* and this is all too *much* and I'm tired, so very tired and—

I feel the force of Miriam's first blow to the door throughout my entire body. A single deadened *thwock* and violent splintering. I catch the silvery tip of an axe blade shark-finning through the door.

"*No*," I murmur.

It takes her but two more impressively efficient strikes to make a hole large enough to shove her hand through and undo the latch. By then, I've already opened the window, swept the snow from the ledge as if I leapt through it, and taken refuge beneath the deepest pile of dolls shoved unceremoniously in the corner. The largest ones the shelves cannot hold.

The smell among the dolls is of old paste, mildew, and a troubling undercurrent of sweat. I work to keep my breaths rhythmic and shallow to avoid both the stench and Miriam's detection.

Through a tiny sliver between a stuffed arm and a burlap cheek, I watch her plod through the snow-moistened carpet. Her skin and hair are drenched with it. She must have had to venture outside for the ax. I'm distantly grateful to see the weapon missing from her hands but the relief is soon replaced by a flicker of movement among the dolls that hide me.

I cannot react. If I do, she'll find me. She has already reached the open window, shaking her head with a chuckle before dragging it closed.

"That was clever, Ceci," she says. "But there is no way you could have withstood a jump from this height."

The dolls' gagged wailing intensifies, reverberating along my flesh. What are they? What has Miriam done to grant them consciousness without free movement? Was that by design? And— I do not linger on this theory long because to do so would rob me of any shred of courage I have left—could they have once been... people?

"Quiet," Miriam says, her voice soft, gentle even.

To my wary surprise, the moans dissipate at her word until the noises have faded entirely. Part of me wishes they would return, if only to cover the sound of my own breathing.

"Come now, Ceci. You cannot possibly hide forever. Come out and speak with me."

She crosses to the bed first, kneeling to check underneath just as I did when trying to locate what I now know was the dolls' moans. As I calculate the likelihood of being able to run past her and take up the ax she dropped, a pale glint catches my eye.

My miniature twin doll, prone and defenseless upon the vanity seat where I left her. My breath catches. Miriam hasn't seen her yet. If I'm quick, I could reach the doll before she does.

With a harried whine, I leap from the tangle of artificial bodies, straight toward the vanity. Miriam is upon me in an instant, bare slender arms wrapped solidly about my waist. Her flesh is cool and moist, but with an inner fire buried underneath. That, coupled with the crush of her breasts against my back brings an unwanted heat to my cheeks.

"It's all right, my lovely," she purrs against the shell of my ear. "There is no need to hide. Not any longer."

Even as I claw and thrash against her, her true meaning does not escape me. That it is not her I was hiding from. Never her. And the bald truth of it holds me in her sway better than her vise-like grip or enchanted dolls ever could.

"We can't, Miri," I say, sagging against her. "You know we can't."

A beat of silence as her arms mercifully slacken. The dolls witness, impassive and dead-eyed, as tears leave their salt taste upon my quivering lips.

Softly, with the care one might handle a fragile thing, she guides my body to face hers. She is the most devastating sight, all the familiar fire leeched from her until she resembles a doll herself, a numb and lifeless shell of the girl I—

"Tell me you do not love me," she says hollowly. "I must hear you say it."

I close my eyes around a jarring sob.

"I do not love you," I blurt and instantly wish I could grasp the poisoned lie from the air and shove it back on my tongue and let it rot me from the inside. As it is, her fallen, crumpled expression is just as punishing. Moreso.

I expect fury. Lunacy. But she does nothing more than close her eyes, the edges of her lips curling into a half smile.

"Thank you," she says. "The storm has ebbed for now. You should hurry home before it picks back up again."

Profound relief and crushing ruin overtake me. After I leave

Everleigh Manor tonight, I will never return. Of that, I am certain. I shall marry Frederick, move to the city and make believe this night was nothing more than some dark fever dream.

Miriam Everleigh was never truly mine.

She's twisted away from me now, shoulders rocking. It takes every ounce of restraint not to run a soothing hand across her bare shoulder blades.

"I am truly sorry," I whisper to her heaving back. She says nothing as I sidestep the ruined splinters of the door. Facing the darkened hallway, I consider turning back as Orpheus did, if only to assure her that I meant what I said before. That I will never speak of this night with anyone. That I forgive her. That I wish—

I hear the shatter before I feel it. A dropped dinner plate. A lilting crack. I fall, striking my head on her marble vanity top. My vision wavers with each of Miriam's steps until she stands over me, the doll in one hand and its porcelain foot in the other. With a dazed whimper, I scan the length of my body and release a ragged mewl at what I find.

My ankle is a perfect twin of the doll's. Bloodless. Jagged edges. My foot rests several inches away inside my lace-up boot, only instead of meat and muscle surrounding a bone core, the limb is hollow. Porcelain. A network of black cracks spiderweb up my calf, ceramic giving way to living tissue.

Miriam kneels beside me, triumphant and smug as if she won yet another round of croquet or outlasted me in a game of hide-and-seek. Even as children, she always won. This time is no differ-ent. She will have her way. She always gets her way.

"Don't be afraid, my lovely," she says. "You can be repaired. This can all be fixed, you'll see."

"Miri..." I moan, stemming the blood flowing down my scalp from my fall. I lift my deformed leg, shuddering at the loss of feeling where my foot once was. Where there should be pain, there is only a dull nothing, heavy as clay. My best friend's eyes are as lifeless as the doll she holds as both stare down at me. She lays the doll's castaway foot on the vanity before regarding me again.

Her other dolls watch with lifeless dispassion, even as their groans and pleas wind through my ringing ears.

"I have always been able to tell when you are lying," Miriam says, her voice achingly tender as she brushes a sweaty strand of hair from my eyes. "You do love me, Cecile. You always have."

We could run away together.

Last year, when her parents still controlled the manor and her fortune. But not her spirit. No one could ever take that from Miriam Everleigh. In the back garden, away from the servants' prying eyes, my damp face buried in her shoulder. Because after weeks of courtship from several would-be suitors, I finally began to understand how my life never truly belonged to me and how powerless I was to stop it.

That was when she said it. Her beautiful, impossible offer.

We could find a little cottage by the sea. Grow herbs and sell them to apothecaries. We could swim in the ocean and chart the stars and watch the ships. Just you and I, my lovely.

The vision twined around my heart and squeezed as we faced each other, hopeful sighs mingling in the air between us. And at that moment, I came to recognize the true reason for my tears. And in my shame and my terror, I reared back and barked out a laugh, pretending her softly spoken, achingly alluring words were nothing more than a jest.

That very evening, I accepted Frederick's proposal.

Broken and at Miriam's mercy, I choke around a sob. She's hurt me. Shattered me.

But God, how I have awoken in the loneliest nights from sweet dreams of her lips on mine, her possessive fingers sliding through my hair, her laughter across my skin. How I have tucked those shameful, torturous fantasies down deep where no one can find them, least of all myself.

"Say it," she urges above my whimpering. "Say it and I will see to it that no one ever hurts you again."

"*You're* hurting me," I weep.

"I am saving you," she says, her voice steady and certain. "You and I... We are inevitable. We always have been. This is my gift to you, Cecile. Admit your truth and we can finally begin our lives. Together."

"I—I don't want..." I stammer, dizzied by converging thoughts of Mother's fury, Miriam's savagery, and the condemnation of a world that will never condone the life Miri and I could have shared. What she is proposing is impossible. She is devastation, this incandescent flame of a woman before me. My most treasured friend. My ruin.

"It's all right. I've got you," says Miriam, pulling me into her lap. I rest my cheek against her stomach, inhaling her as she holds me against the pain she caused.

The doll's curls tickle my face, its expression heartbreakingly sad. My mirror. My gift.

"Miriam," I say, closing my eyes. "Miri..."

"Yes," she says with feeling. "Yes, I'm here. I will always be here."

Hot tears in my eyes, I bundle the front of her dress in my fist and drag her face to mine. Our lips collide with a gentle impact before I part her lips with my tongue, tasting her. She groans into my mouth, our salty tears mingling as we kiss our collected pain away, banishing the world and its barriers to places so far off they can never trap us again.

"I love you," I whisper with an exhale that sounds terribly like a gentle breeze over ocean waves. Like one might hear ensconced within a cozy cottage by the sea... "I will always love you."

My dearest friend rattles out a sigh as my fingers grasp the doll's arm.

With her eyes trained on mine, her smile cast in all the radiance of the spring sunshine over the wildflower fields in which we played, I lift the doll and dash her porcelain face against the ground.

EPILOGUE

Three winters come and go. We share her canopy bed, the floor-to-ceiling shelves of dolls watching over us while we sleep. A sea of baked clay, fabric, glass, wax, and gleaming eyes of all shapes and sizes. Miriam's lifelong collection. Most are comfortingly silent and inanimate, but sometimes, I can hear the others.

Lord and Lady Everleigh. Horrible old Mrs. Stark. Their close-mouthed moans, the wordless pleas that no longer hold any horror for me.

My new body has never once touched that pile. I am not like the others, that lifeless throng. I am singular. Miri's finest work. We are never apart, she and I. As promised, she has saved me. Repaired me. Protected me. Her favorite toy. She spares hardly a glance at the others anymore. Her collection stopped with me.

Tonight, she has moved me into our sitting room beneath the light of the immense evergreen tree and its usual adornments. She folds my immobile hands in my lap, the cracks in my glossy skin faint as gossamer lace. She has dressed me in a fine green gown, polished my face with rose water, and draped emeralds around my neck.

"Happy Christmas, my lovely," she says, her lips warm against a deep rift marring the surface of my cheek. Humming beneath her breath, she takes up a brush and glides its bristles through my golden hair. With a shifting sound of stone sliding against stone, I close my eyes. My heart beats, the meaty organ pumping like a whisper beneath my ceramic exterior.

A bead of moisture gathers at the corner of my glass eye and vanishes into my vast network of fractures before Miri can see it.

Happy Christmas, my Miri.

I will always love you.

ACKNOWLEDGMENTS

Thank you to my fantastic editors D.L. Winchester and Rebecca Cuthbert for your keen eyes and insight. To my early readers who got to enjoy this book when it was just a 3,500 short story, I cannot thank you enough for your kind words while you cheered on this project's expansion. To Eric—while there is so much to love about you, the fact that you don't have a horrifying doll collection is now pretty high on your list of desirable qualities. To my family, my writing community, and of course, *you*. Thank you for picking up this book and I'm sorry about the doll pile.

ABOUT THE AUTHOR

Chloe York, an award-winning abstract painter, insect taxidermist, and owner of a small oddities company, resides in Birmingham, Alabama with her sculptor husband and ferocious daughter in their shared home and studio. When she's not painting seascapes or framing bugs, she can be found in her lair writing fantasy and horror novels.

Author Website: www.chloe-york.com

instagram.com/chloe.york.art

facebook.com/chloe.york

If you are a fan of horror stories and tales, you'll want to follow
Undertaker Books.
We're bringing you stories to take to your grave.